If Dinosaurs Lived in My Town

If Dinosaurs Lived in My Town

Written by
Marianne Plumridge

Illustrated by
Bob Eggleton

Sky Pony Press • New York

For Mum and Dad,
Margaret and Eric Plumridge,
Who always believed I could . . .

Mari

For Dad,
Who introduced me to dinosaurs,
And for Mom, who found Godzilla . . .
And to Ray Harryhausen, the man who made me see dinosaurs walk.

Bob

What if . . .

Everyone knows just a little bit about dinosaurs—a snippet about what they were, when they lived, and when they might have died. They were reptiles; big, lumbering reptiles and also quick little reptiles. Some were bird-like and others were lizard-like. And millions and millions of years ago, they covered the planet—way before the history of humans began.

Then something happened and all the dinosaurs died. We don't know how or why. But ever since the first fossils were found, scientists have tried to find out.

What we know about dinosaurs comes from years and years of study. Bones and fossils dug up all over the world are carefully put together again like a giant jigsaw puzzle. Sometimes all the pieces are there, but most often they are not. Then the scientists have to think hard about what that dinosaur *might* have looked like. To do this, they see what other members of the dinosaur's family looked like and then compare them.

But what if the dinosaurs never died out millions of years ago? What if they still lived today? What if they lived right here in my town . . .

If a Corythosaurus lived in my town . . .

. . . she could be a crossing guard.

Dinosaur Factprint!

Corythosaurus (ko-rith-oh-saw-rus) was large, colorful, and crested. She could walk upright on her long, sturdy back legs. At twice the height of a human adult, she would be large enough to stop traffic and colorful enough to not need the neon vests that school crossing guards or road crews wear. *Corythosaurus's* snout was shaped like a duck's bill, and instead of regular teeth, she had hundreds of little teeth inside of her cheeks to chew with.

If a Rhamphorhynchus lived in my town . . .

Dinosaur Factprint!

Rhamphorhynchus (ram-for-rink-us) means "beak snout." He was a flying reptile. His beak contained many sharp, fang-like teeth that stuck out at an angle from his long, narrow jaw. Many squirming, slithery fish could be easily caught or speared when this fish-hunter skimmed the surface of the water. Scientists now think that *Rhamphorhynchus* might have had a throat pouch, like a pelican, for holding its prey.

. . . we would catch the most fish!

. . . he could live
in his own house
in the backyard!

BAMBI

Dinosaur Factprint!

Bambiraptor (bam-bee-rap-tor) was a member of a group of very small, very fast, meat-eating dinosaurs called "dino-birds." Although he looked very birdlike—with his covering of downy fluff, feathered arms, and sharp claws—he was still very much a dinosaur. He was about the size of a turkey, had long, sharp teeth, and equally long, sharp toe-claws. He could run very fast after much smaller prey. Even though he had feathers, scientists don't believe that *Bambiraptor* could fly. He was, however, a very good tree climber.

Dinosaur Factprint!

Stegosaurus (steg-oh-saw-rus) means "roof lizard." She was named that because when the first *Stegosaurus* skeleton was found, the scientists didn't know how the dinosaur's big bony spine plates were attached. They thought they were some kind of flat, protective armor. It wasn't until much later that they found out that the broad, leaf-shaped plates really stood upright in two rows along the dinosaur's back and tail.

. . . we could climb on her plates like a jungle gym!

If a Tyrannosaurus Rex lived in my town . .

14

. . . he would take a lot of cleaning up after!

Dinosaur Factprint!

Tyrannosaurus rex (tie-ran-oh-saw-rus recks) means "king of the tyrant lizards." Standing at three times the height of a human adult, *T. rex* (tee-recks) was one of the biggest meat-eating animals to ever walk the earth. Scientists have found lots of dinosaur poop fossils. They call these fossils "coprolites." Scientists study coprolites to find out what different dinosaurs liked to eat and even how they ate it. One of the biggest coprolites found so far came from a young *T. rex*. That coprolite was about the size of a loaf of bread, only longer. That big dino poop would surely clog your toilet!

Dinosaur Factprint!

Parasaurolophus (pa-ra-saw-roh-loff-us) was a very striking dinosaur, about the size of a small bus. On his head he had a hollow, bony crest that was over six feet long. He could blow air through this tube to make a variety of noises that sounded like notes played on a French horn, or even a deep-noted trombone or bassoon. *Parasaurolophus* might have made these noises to raise an alarm, warn off rivals, or to attract a mate.

. . . he could join
our marching band!

. . . she could swim with the whales in the aquarium for exercise!

18

Dinosaur Factprint!

Liopleurodon (lee-oh-ploor-oh-don) lived in the ocean and had four very big flippers. The front flippers most likely moved up and down, while the back flippers were used in a kicking motion. *Liopleurodon* was the biggest meat-eater the world has ever known. Even bigger than the Blue Whale that swims in our seas today! She looked somewhat like a modern whale, but had a huge head that took up at least one quarter of her entire body length. That's about the full size of most dinosaurs!

Dinosaur Factprint!

Maiasaura (may-ah-saw-ra) means "good-earth mother lizard." People believe that she was a caring, family-loving dinosaur. Although she's quite huge—30 feet long and twice the height of a human adult—she would be very gentle with tiny human children. A baby *Maiasaura* wouldn't be much bigger than you!

. . . then having a babysitter
would be so much more fun.

Dinosaur Factprint!

Giganotosaurus (gig-an-oh-toe-saw-rus) means "giant southern lizard." He is the largest meat-eating land dinosaur ever discovered. His skull was about 6 feet long. That's equal to the same height of a tall human adult! Some of *Giganotosaurus's* teeth were at least 5 inches long and razor-sharp like a shark's teeth. Scientists believe that he slashed sideways at prey with his teeth rather than charging and biting head on.

. . . he would need a really big toothbrush!

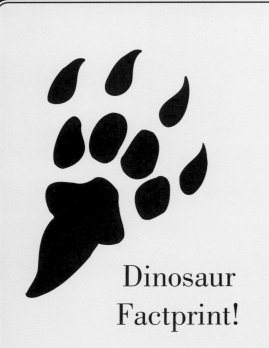

Dinosaur Factprint!

Tarbosaurus (tar-boh-saw-rus) is a close cousin of the *Tyrannosaurus Rex*, and even looks very much like him. They didn't eat regular meals like us. They would stuff themselves at one meal and then not eat again for a few days. Each dinosaur would have eaten his own weight in meat every week— that's about 60,000 hamburgers!

. . he and his cousin, Tyrannosaurus Rex,
could have a hamburger
eating contest!

TARBIE

Dinosaur Factprint!

Styracosaurus (sty-rak-oh-saw-rus) means "spiked lizard." She had a very large neck frill with six long spikes around the edge, and lots of smaller spikes too. She also had a very big horn on her nose—at least 2 feet long. It's very likely that it was used to protect herself from other dinosaurs. Many people believe that the frill and face of *Styracosaurus* was brightly colored.

. . . she would have a huge birthday cake just to hold all of the candles. And she's already wearing a party hat!

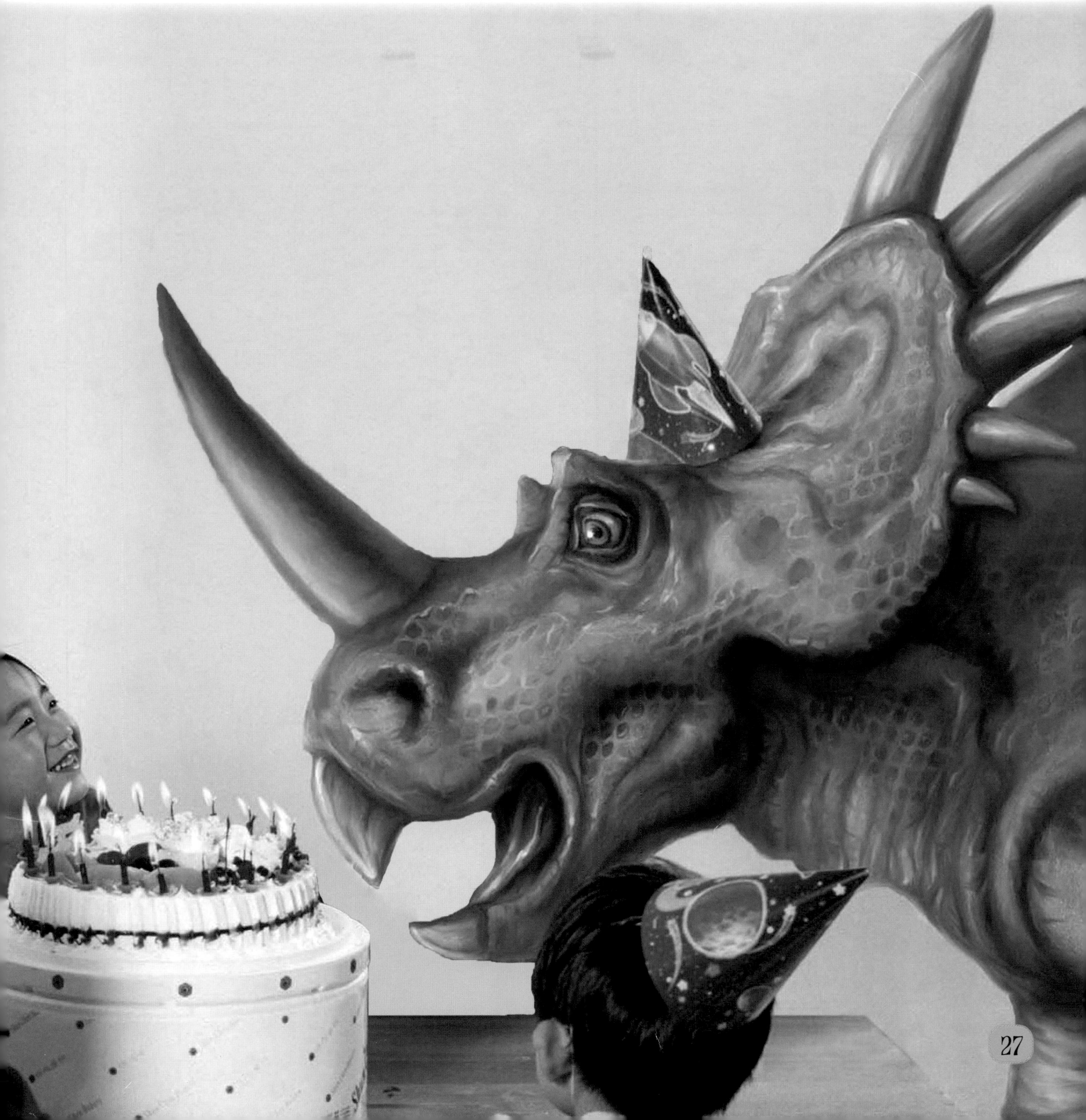

. . . we could play catch, but he'd have to be careful that his claws didn't pop the ball!

Dinosaur Factprint!

Velociraptor (vel-o-see-rap-tor) means "fast hunter." He is probably the best known dinosaur of the raptor family, as well as one of the fiercest of all dinosaurs. He had three very sharp claws on each big hand and on each foot. On the second toe of each foot was a terrible, half-moon shaped claw. *Velociraptor* also had 80 very sharp, jagged teeth. He was a very dangerous dino!

If a Pteranodon lived in my town . . .

. . . we could go
hang gliding!

Dinosaur Factprint!

Pteranodon (ter-an-oh-don) means "wing without teeth." He was a great glider with a very large wingspan. However, due to hollow bones, he only weighed about 40 pounds. Instead of a tail, he had a short, pointy nub. But his head was almost as long as his body! He had a long pointy beak and was topped by an equally large, pointy head-crest.

Dinosaur Factprint!

Ornithomimus (or-nith-oh-meem-us) means "bird mimic." He was a tall, skinny dinosaur. He was around the same size and looked very much like a modern ostrich, but had no feathers. He had long powerful legs, long thin arms, a beak, and no teeth. He could run very, very fast—as much as 30 miles per hour!`

. . . he'd win every race.

If a Supersaurus lived in my town . . .

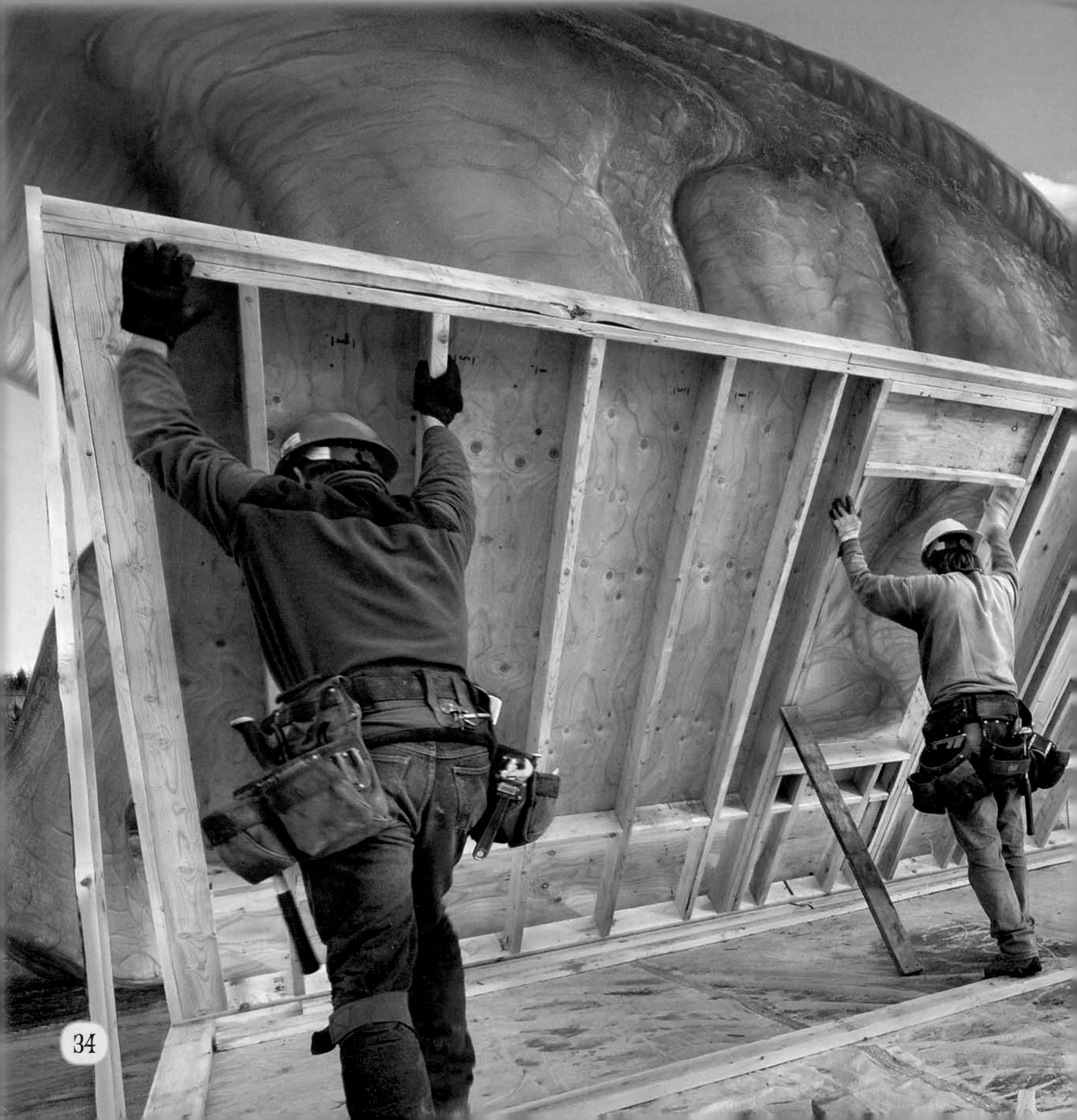

Dinosaur Factprint!

Supersaurus means "super lizard." She was one of the biggest dinosaurs and had an incredibly long neck and tail. Four big, elephant-like legs supported her large size and weight, and helped balance her when she searched for food in tall trees. She measured 98 feet long, which is like 7 big cars parked bumper-to-bumper.

. . . she could help build houses.

Dinosaur Factprint!

Talarurus (ta-la-ru-rus) means "wicker tail." He was a small dinosaur who wore lots of armor. He had many bony plates on his flat back and lots of pointy knobs. He looked very thorny. His best feature, though, was his tail. It was long, thin, and very stiff, and had a big bony knot on the end. He could thwack other dinos with it!

. . . he could hit a home run every time!

38

. . . she would have the biggest eggs in the barnyard!

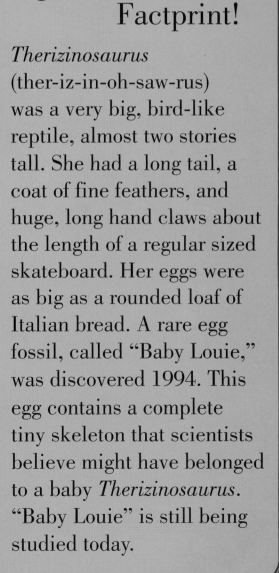

Dinosaur Factprint!

Therizinosaurus (ther-iz-in-oh-saw-rus) was a very big, bird-like reptile, almost two stories tall. She had a long tail, a coat of fine feathers, and huge, long hand claws about the length of a regular sized skateboard. Her eggs were as big as a rounded loaf of Italian bread. A rare egg fossil, called "Baby Louie," was discovered 1994. This egg contains a complete tiny skeleton that scientists believe might have belonged to a baby *Therizinosaurus*. "Baby Louie" is still being studied today.

. . . he could be a spaghetti chef!

Dinosaur Factprint!

Deinonychus (die-non-ee-kus) means "terrible claw." He was a thin, bird-like dinosaur that stood as tall as a modern day basketball player. He had large hands with three sharp claws on each, and was a smart dinosaur. *Deinonychus* would have been very fast and skilled at twirling and separating tangled things—like spaghetti!

If a Brachiosaurus lived in my town . . .

Paris in the Spring

POST CARD

. . . she would bring back super-sized vacation pictures.

re Sunny Italy

t Mount Rushmore

Dinosaur Factprint!

Brachiosaurus means "arm lizard." She was one of the very tallest dinosaurs. Although she was bigger than a giraffe, and had a long tail, she looked like a huge reptile version of a giraffe with her high shoulders, low backside, long neck, and small head. However, *Brachiosaurus* would be very small compared to the Eiffel Tower in Paris. The Leaning Tower of Pisa in Italy would be three times as tall as her, while a Gondola boat would only be as long as her neck and head.

Dinosaur Factprint!

Pachycephalosaurus (pack-ee-sef-al-oh-saw-rus) means "thick-headed lizard." He was the biggest of the "bone-headed" dinosaurs. No, he wasn't stubborn. It means that he had a very solid skull—10 inches thick at the top. That's about the height of a plastic milk bottle! He walked upright on his heavy back legs and was very fast on his feet.

. . . he could come biking with us and he wouldn't need a helmet!

If a Torosaurus lived in my town . . .

. . . we could use him as a chair and have the best view of the fireworks.

Dinosaur Factprint!

Torosaurus (tore-oh-saw-rus) means "punctured lizard." He had the biggest head of any land-living animal—it was over 8 feet long! It was so big because of his enormous neck shield. He was a strong dinosaur, was about the size of a bus, and walked on four thick, sturdy legs. His face had three horns for protection—two big, long ones over the eyes and one small one above his beaked nose.

Dinosaur Factprint!

Peteinosaurus (pet-ine-oh-saw-rus) means "winged lizard." He was a tiny flying dinosaur. About the size of a well-fed pigeon, and with a similar size wingspan, he had a long, thin tail with a leaf-shaped paddle at the end. The paddle helped to steer while flying. *Peteinosaurus's* head was made up of mostly his beak and large eyes.

. . . we wouldn't have bird feeders; we'd have tiny dino feeders!

If a Coelophysis lived in my town . . .

Dinosaur Factprint!

Coelophysis (see-low-fie-sis) means "hollow form." He was a skinny, fast-moving dinosaur that, when standing on his hind legs, was as tall as a human adult. A fossilized *Coelophysis* skull was flown into space by the Space Shuttle *Endeavor* in 1998. For a short time, it stayed on the Mir Space Station, before coming back home to Earth.

. . . he could go into space. Oh, wait— one of them already has!

If a Euoplocephalus lived in my town . . .

. . . he would break a piñata with one swipe of his tail!

Dinosaur Factprint!

Euoplocephalus (you-oh-plo-sef-ah-luss) means "well armored head." He was like a small armored truck, with lots of bony plates and studs covering his back. He also had a long tail with a heavy bone knot at the end of it. He could swing his tail like a club to defend himself, or to smash trees to bring branches low enough to nibble on leaves if he got tired of munching on ground plants.

If a Cryolophosaurus lived in my town . . .

Dinosaur Factprint!

Cryolophosaurus (cry-oh-loff-oh-saw-rus) means "frozen crested lizard." She was called that because her bones were found at the South Pole. She was a medium-sized dinosaur, about 25 feet long. She had a large head, half of which was a long mouth filled with very sharp teeth. An unusual, fancy crest sat on top of her head and made her look very festive.

. . . she could be a circus star.

If a Leaellynasaura lived in my town . . .

Dinosaur Factprint!

Leaellynasaura (lee-el-in-ah-saw-rah) was named after the discoverer's daughter and means "Leaellyn's female lizard." *Leaellynasaura* was a skinny little dinosaur that lived in the ancient ice and snow of the South Pole. She had huge eyes to see in the long, dark winter months there, as well as a large brain.

. . . we could read together in the dark.

If dinosaurs lived
in my town . . .

. . . we would need
a BIGGER town!

References

Dinosaurs and Prehistoric Life (Smithsonian Handbooks) by Hazel Richardson. A Dorling Kindersley Book, 2003.

The Ultimate Dinosaur Book by David Lambert. Dorling Kindersley, in association with The Natural History Museum, London, 1993.

The Complete Book of Dinosaurs by Dougal Dixon. Hermes House, London, 2006.

National Geographic Dinosaurs by Paul Barrett and illustrated by Raul Martin. National Geographic Society, Washington, DC, 1999, 2000.

The Macmillan Illustrated Encyclopedia of Dinosaurs and Prehistoric Animals by Dougla Dixon, Barry Cox, R. J. G. Savage, and Brian Gardiner. Macmillan, New York, 1988.

About the author

Marianne Plumridge is an artist, writer, and book reviewer for the Science Fiction, Fantasy, and Mystery genres. Her artwork has graced magazine covers, greeting cards, jigsaw puzzles, and the occasional book, while her essays, fiction, and book reviews have gained respect and recognition on the Internet and also in print.

Ms. Plumridge also shares a condo with her husband, Bob Eggleton, and several thousand "kaiju" monsters, dinosaurs, dragons, and other beasties in the form of toys and figurines, as well as books and movies. Inspiration is never lost for long.

About the illustrator

Bob Eggleton is a Science Fiction and Fantasy artist and lecturer. He has seven art books and illustrated works to his credit, one of which won the 2001 Hugo Award for Best Related book. Mr. Eggleton has also received eight Hugo Awards for Best Professional Artist, Locus Awards, the Skylark Award, Chesley Awards, Analog and Asimov Magazine Awards, among others, throughout his longstanding art career.

In addition, Mr. Eggleton has a wide-ranging knowledge of dinosaurs and other prehistoric animals, which led him to a lifelong interest in big monsters and monster films from around the world. Not only has he painted and illustrated these favorite subjects, but Mr. Eggleton has also given lectures and written essays and articles about them for publication. This includes writing and illustrating an issue of a Godzilla comic for Dark Horse Comics in 1996, as well as illustrating many monster comic and magazine covers for them. In the film industry he was a Conceptual Artist for *Star Trek*, the Nickelodeon film *Jimmy Neutron Boy Genius* (2001), and Warner Bros' *The Ant Bully* (2006).

He was also an extra in a Godzilla film in 2002, and continues to be an honored guest at Toho Studios whenever he is in Japan.

Index